Unbelievable Pictures and Facts About Lacrosse

By: Olivia Greenwood

Introduction

There are so many fun and exciting facts about Lacrosse, that you could sit and learn about it forever. We are going to try and provide you with an overview of some of the most important facts and information about Lacrosse.

What exactly does a game of Lacrosse entail?

Lacrosse is a particular type of team sport that is played in a very big field. There are two teams that play against one another. Players make use of a very special stick called a crosse that has a net pocket that is able to catch the ball, throw the ball, scoop the balls and carry the ball. The aim of the game is to score points by getting the ball into the opponent's net.

Where is Lacrosse the most popular?

Although the game is growing in popularity all over the world, it is considered to be the most popular in the United States of America.

Do we know who invented the game or not?

If we trace back the history of the game it is said that lacrosse dates back to the 1100s. The game was said to have been first played and invented by the Native North American people.

Was Lacrosse used in the past for anything in particular?

Lacrosse was actually used for a couple of different things many years ago. A different version of lacrosse without all the rules and regulations that it has today was used in order to prepare boys for the war. It was also used in 1763 as a distraction technique to distract the British soldiers.

Is Lacrosse currently a part of the Olympic games?

Lacrosse is not currently a part of the Olympics Games. However, it has been part of the Olympics games many years ago. It later became a demonstration sport. People all over the world are holding thumbs that the game will be a part of the Olympics games in the future.

Have the teams in Lacrosse always been the same amount?

The amount of people in the lacrosse teams has not always been the amount that it is today. In today's times, there are ten players on each team. Many years ago there were often thousands of players involved in one game.

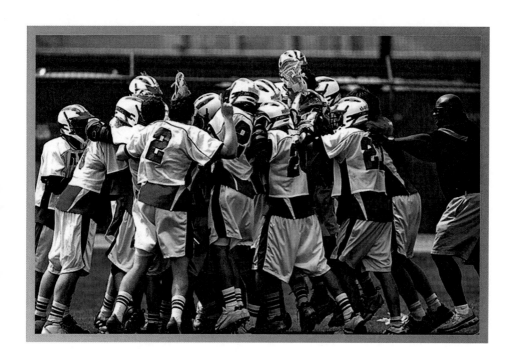

Why is Lacrosse considered to be such a unique sport?

This game is extremely unique for many reasons, but what makes it exceptionally unique is that it is made up of a combination of other sports. The game is made up of soccer, hockey, and basketball all combined together.

Is the sport of Lacrosse a dangerous one?

In comparison to other sports, lacrosse is not considered to be too dangerous. Although it is common for players to experience minor injuries such as cuts and bruises. It is also a game that takes protection very seriously and there are lots of safety measures in place to ensure that players don't get hurt.

Is Lacrosse considered to be a fast game or not?

The answer is a big yes as lacrosse is considered to be a very fast game. In fact, it is actually known to many people as the fastest game that is played on two feet. Sometimes the ball can travel so fast in the game, that you can even miss seeing it if you are watching.

What are some of the basic rules of Lacrosse?

The game has quite a couple of rules that you will get more familiar with as you play the game. The ball is not allowed to touch the player's hands at all. There are ten players who can be on each team. There needs to be three attack players, three middies, three defenders, and one goalie on each team. These are just some of the many basic rules of the game.

Has Lacrosse always had the same name?

The game has not always been known as lacrosse. Many years back it was known as stickball and later on the name changed to lacrosse as we know it today.

Who is the only person who is allowed to touch the ball with their hands?

The rules of the game indicate that only one person is allowed to touch the ball with their hands and this rule applies only to the goalie.

Is Lacrosse a good game for children to play?

Lacrosse is actually an excellent game for children to play for many reasons. Not only are there many physical benefits but there are also many social benefits. This is besides the fact that the game helps children to learn discipline, patience, and much more. It helps children to learn how to communicate with all sorts of people from diverse backgrounds. The list of benefits of playing lacrosse is long.

What is harder to play Lacrosse or baseball?

Many people may not know the answer to this question, but today you will discover the answer. After a couple of discussions, it has been concluded that baseball is actually a harder game to learn how to play than lacrosse.

Is there a good age to start playing Lacrosse?

There is certainly a good age to start playing the game and this is at the age of ten or eleven years old.

Do boys and girls play the game of lacrosse?

In the past, the game was only played by males but over the years females have also learned to play the game. Now the game is played by both males and females.

Where is a good place to learn how to play Lacrosse?

One of the best places to learn how to play lacrosse is at school. Many schools across the world and especially in the United States have lacrosse teams that you can join.

Is Lacrosse becoming increasingly popular?

Lacrosse is a sport that is continuously growing in popularity. It is becoming increasingly popular all over the world every single year. At this current point in time, it is considered to be the number one growing sport in America.

What are considered to be fouls in Lacrosse?

In Lacrosse, you get different types of fouls. There personal fouls and technical fouls. Technical fouls include things like stalling, pushing, and not having the correct number of players on each side. Personal fouls include things like tripping, aggressiveness, slashing, or even making contact with other players while the stick is still between your hands.

What happens if someone commits five personal fouls?

If someone commits five personal fouls in lacrosse, the same thing happens to them just like it does in a basketball match. The player is removed from the game and won't be able to finish playing that particular game.

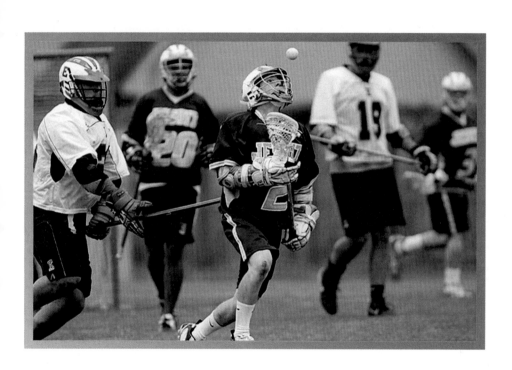

Made in United States
North Haven, CT
17 October 2022

25583336R00024